little
Miss
Somersault

by Roger Hargreaves

Little Miss Somersault is the sort of person who doesn't just go out for a walk.

Oh no, not Little Miss Somersault.

She is too full of energy for that.

Rather than walking everywhere,
she cartwheels everywhere!

She doesn't just walk through her front door.

That would be too easy.

She built a house where she could climb
over the roof first!

Little Miss Somersault doesn't just
sit in a chair.

She balances on the back of it.

Little Miss Somersault doesn't
walk around things.

She jumps right over them!

And rather than answer the telephone like you or I might, she...

...well, just look at her!

The other day, when she was cartwheeling past Mr Worry's house, he called out to her. "There's a leaf on my roof. Please could you get it for me?" he asked.

Mr Worry had spent the whole morning worrying that the leaf might make his roof fall in!

"I have a long ladder," he added.

Little Miss Somersault said, "I don't need a ladder." And, quick as a flash, she climbed on top of Mr Worry's house and got the leaf off.

A little further down the lane,
Little Miss Somersault came to
Mr Skinny's house.

Mr Skinny was at the top of a ladder,
painting his roof.

Unfortunately, Mr Bump came around the corner and walked under the ladder.

Or rather, he tried to walk under the ladder, but being Mr Bump he walked straight into it.

BUMP!

And you can see what happened!

Little Miss Somersault had seen it all happen.

And without a thought for the ladder lying on
the ground, she climbed to the top of
Mr Skinny's house and carried him
safely to the ground,
under her arm.

He wasn't very heavy!

By the next morning, everybody had heard
about Little Miss Somersault's daring deeds.

The phone rang. It was Mr Uppity.
"There's an umbrella stuck in my chimney.
I hear you're good at climbing onto roofs.
I'll expect you here in five minutes!"

Mr Uppity's house is one of the biggest
houses you will ever have seen.

"To climb to the top of Mr Uppity's house
would be a real challenge," said
Little Miss Somersault.

It took no time at all for Little Miss Somersault
to climb on to Mr Uppity's roof.

"That was easy," she said, as she
balanced on a chimney pot.

Then she looked down at the ground, far below her.

That was the last thing she should have done.
Little Miss Somersault suddenly felt dizzy.
Her knees began to tremble.
Everything began to spin round and round.

Little Miss Somersault had discovered she
was afraid of heights!

Luckily, Mr Tickle happened to be passing.

He stretched out one of his
extraordinarily long arms.

Do you think he wanted to tickle
Little Miss Somersault?

Of course he did!

But not before he had brought her back
safely down to the ground.

"Stop it!" laughed Little Miss Somersault.
"I promise I won't do anything so foolish again!"

And off went Mr Tickle to look for
somebody else to tickle.

That evening, Little Miss Somersault was sitting, that's right, sitting, in her armchair.

Suddenly the telephone rang.

"My hat has blown off," said a voice at the other end. "And it's landed on the roof of my house. Could you..."

Little Miss Somersault's face turned pale.

"Who is this?" she asked, in a trembling voice.

"It's Mr Small," said Mr Small.

Little Miss Somersault breathed a
huge sigh of relief.

"I'll be there in five minutes!" she said.

And off she somersaulted!

Fantastic offers for Little Miss fans!

Collect all your Mr. Men or Little Miss books in these superb durable collectors' cases!
Only £5.99 inc. postage and packing, these wipe-clean, hard-wearing cases will give all your Mr. Men or Little Miss books a beautiful new home!

Keep track of your collection with this giant-sized double-sided Mr. Men and Little Miss Collectors' poster.
Collect 6 tokens and we will send you a brilliant giant-sized double-sided collectors' poster! Simply tape a £1 coin to cover postage and packing in the space provided and fill out the form overleaf.

STICK £1 COIN HERE
(for poster only)

Only need a few Little Miss or Mr. Men to complete your set? You can order any of the titles on the back of the books from our Mr. Men order line on 0870 787 1724. Orders should be delivered between 5 and 7 working days.

─────── TO BE COMPLETED BY AN ADULT ───────

To apply for any of these great offers, ask an adult to complete the details below and send this whole page with the appropriate payment and tokens, to: MR. MEN CLASSIC OFFER, PO BOX 715, HORSHAM RH12 5WG

☐ Please send me a giant-sized double-sided collectors' poster.

AND ☐ I enclose 6 tokens and have taped a £1 coin to the other side of this page.

☐ Please send me ☐ Mr. Men Library case(s) and/or ☐ Little Miss library case(s) at £5.99 each inc P&P

☐ I enclose a cheque/postal order payable to Egmont UK Limited for £....................................

OR ☐ Please debit my MasterCard / Visa / Maestro / Delta account (delete as appropriate) for £....................................

Card no. ☐☐☐☐☐☐☐☐☐☐☐☐☐☐☐☐☐☐☐ Security code ☐☐☐

Issue no. (if available) ☐ Start Date ☐☐/☐☐/☐☐ Expiry Date ☐☐/☐☐/☐☐

Fan's name: .... Date of birth: ....

Address: ....

....

Postcode: ....

Name of parent / guardian: ....

Email for parent / guardian: ....

Signature of parent / guardian: ....

Please allow 28 days for delivery. Offer is only available while stocks last. We reserve the right to change the terms of this offer at any time and we offer a 14 day money back guarantee. This does not affect your statutory rights. Offers apply to UK only.

☐ We may occasionally wish to send you information about other Egmont children's books. If you would rather we didn't, please tick this box. **Ref: LIM 001**

cut along the dotted line and return this whole page